BLOOMSBURY
CHILDREN'S BOOKS
Bloomsbury Publishing Plc
50 Bedford Square, London, WC1B 3DP, UK
29 Earlsfort Terrace, Dublin 2, Ireland

BLOOMSBURY, BLOOMSBURY CHILDREN'S BOOKS
and the Diana logo are trademarks of Bloomsbury Publishing Plc

978 1 5266 3259 3 (HB)
978 1 5266 3253 1 (eBook)

First published in Great Britain 2022 by Bloomsbury Publishing Plc

Text and illustrations copyright © Debi Gliori 2022

13 5 7 9 10 8 6 4 2

Debi Gliori has asserted her right under the
Copyright, Design and Patents Act, 1988,
to be identified as the Author
and Illustrator of this work.

A catalogue record for this book is available
from the British Library

Printed in Italy

To find out more about
our authors and books visit
www.bloomsbury.com
and sign up for our newsletters

For my dearest Viking friends, women o'da Nort;
Noelle A, Mary B and Joyce G. Mightier than any
Dinnhorn, and every bit as brave as Wilma –
this one is for you with my love.
– D.G.

MIX
Paper | Supporting
responsible forestry
FSC
www.fsc.org
FSC® C023419

Wilma the BRAVE

← ─ DEBI GLIORI ─ →

BLOOMSBURY
CHILDREN'S BOOKS
LONDON OXFORD NEW YORK NEW DELHI SYDNEY

Wilma was last-but-one in a family of fearsome Viking warriors. Wilma had **big** plans. She was going to

sail
the
seven
seas,

slay the Monster of the Deep,

and be home in time to read Harald his bedtime saga.

Wilma's brothers roared with laughter.
Wilma was just a girl, they said. Didn't she know anything?
Boys do all the important stuff, they explained.

Boys make big plans, go sailing and slay monsters.
Girls, on the other hand ...

... but Wilma wasn't listening.
It was time for Harald's
bedtime saga.

Then there was
stinkfish to cook,

dishes to
wash, and ...

... menfolk's **underpants** to darn.

"**This is _so_ dull,**" groaned Wilma, as she chopped and darned.

"*So* BORING," she sighed, as she washed and dried and—

Hang on! thought Wilma. *Where is Harald?*

Baby Harald had listened to his big brothers explaining all about boys. He had **no idea** how to sail the seven seas, or slay the Monster of the Deep, but he hoped he'd be back in time for Wilma's bedtime saga.

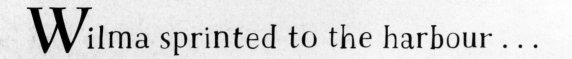

W ilma sprinted to the harbour ...

... just as a gust of wind filled the longship's sails
and sent it (and Harald) far out into the waves.

"Oh no!" shrieked Wilma.
"Sound the Dinnhorn!
Baby at sea!"

She grabbed the horn, but earlier that day a hedgehog had crawled inside it and couldn't crawl back out.

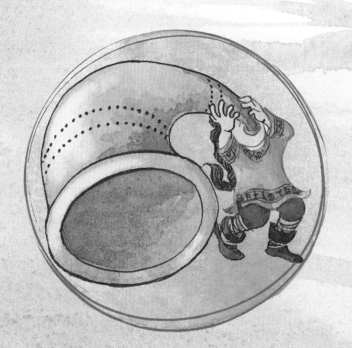

Wilma blew as hard as she could but not a sound would come out of it.
It was no longer a Dinnhorn.
It was a Hushhorn!

There was no way to summon help. And **no time to lose.**

Wilma seized a shield, leaped into the water and using the Hushhorn as a paddle . . .

Hang on, Harald!

. . . rowed for hours and hours, wave after wave,

Don't let go!

not stopping until,
at last,

she caught up
with the baby.

Harald wasn't enjoying his adventure. He was cold
and wet and homesick. However, he was **very** pleased
to see Wilma. Wilma tied the longship to an ice floe
and wrapped Harald and herself snug in the sail.

"Saga time?" asked Harald.
"Saga time," said Wilma.
Harald snuggled closer.

Under a darkening sky, Wilma told a tale of salty seas
and westering winds, and wild girls who flew dragons
by the light of the Aurora to rescue homesick boys.
Soon they were both fast asleep, rocked by a gentle sea.

In the morning, Harald's tummy told a saga all of its own.
"Hungry," said Harald.

"I hear you," said Wilma.

She cut holes in the ice, baited all the longship's oars
and waited.

In the distance, a polar bear waited too.
Hungry, thought the polar bear, gazing at the children.

The ice creaked under him.

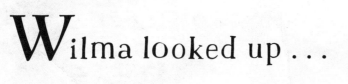

Wilma looked up . . .

and the bear began to **run,**

faster and **faster,** coming **closer** and **closer,** its giant claws digging into the ice.

Wilma snatched Harald up and fled
to the longship.

But the oars had been snapped and broken by the bear!
So once again, Wilma grabbed the Hushhorn
and began to row and row.

But Hushhorns aren't very good for rowing.

And hungry bears can swim very fast.

The bear opened its mouth and stretched
a giant paw toward the children.

But Wilma was no ordinary child.
She had **big** plans.
She had **seas** to sail and **monsters** to slay.
She did not intend to be eaten by a bear.
She raised the Hushhorn high.

"Begone, beast!
Back to the deep!
Away with you!"

The polar bear blinked,
but **kept coming.**

"Don't say I didn't warn you!" roared Wilma, and she **bashed** the bear **hard** on the nose with the Hushhorn.

Inside the Hushhorn, the hedgehog came **unstuck,**

and **fell,** quills first, onto the polar bear's tender nose.

At first, the polar bear
only grunted. Then it
roared.

AAAWWWOOOOOOOOO!

It pawed at its nose.

AIIEEE!
AIIEEE!
AIIEEE!

Blurbbbble
Blurbbbble

Then it dived underwater,
and disappeared.

Wilma rescued the hedgehog, fixed the oars,
collected the fish she'd caught and set sail for home.
Harald sighed with happiness. He'd had enough of sailing
the seven seas and fighting Monsters from the Deep.

He had **big** plans.
Harald planned . . .

. . . to stay home and
make woolly things
to keep his family warm.

To cook a stinkfish stew
so **delicious** everyone
would want seconds.

And **best of all . . .**

. . . Harald was going to invent an
automatic washer-of-dishes
because—as everyone knows—washing
dishes is **very** boring indeed.

Wilma couldn't agree more.
She had **big** plans of her own
and they didn't include
washing dishes.

Wilma was going to travel
to the **Ends** of the **Earth**, via the **Milky Way,**

learn to **fly** with **dragons** by the light of the Aurora . . .

. . . and be home in time
to tell Harald **all** about it.

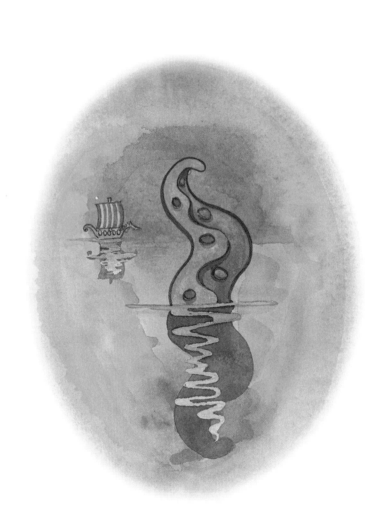